panda series

**PANDA books are for first readers
beginning to make their own way
through books.**

Conor's Concert

GILLIAN PERDUE

· Pictures by Michael Connor ·

THE O'BRIEN PRESS
DUBLIN

First published 2003 by The O'Brien Press Ltd,
20 Victoria Road, Dublin 6, Ireland.
Tel: +353 1 4923333; Fax: +353 1 4922777
E-mail: books@obrien.ie
Website: www.obrien.ie
Reprinted 2006.

ISBN 10: 0-86278-847-1
ISBN 13: 978-0-86278-847-6

British Library Cataloguing-in-Publication Data
Perdue, Gillian
Conor's concert
1.Pianists - Juvenile fiction
2.Composers - Juvenile fiction 3.Children's stories
I.Title
823.9'2[J]

2 3 4 5 6 7 8 9 10
06 07 08 09 10

Typesetting, layout, editing, design: The O'Brien Press Ltd
Printing: Cox & Wyman Ltd

Can YOU spot the panda
hidden in the story?

Conor loved music.
He listened to the radio
when he was in the car
and he hummed or sang along.

In the house, he always put
CDs on the CD player.
He listened to the music
while he played
or did his homework.

And when there was
no music playing,
Conor made up
his own songs.

Music made
Conor's hands happy
and his feet frisky.
It made his heart beat faster
and it made him
want to jump around.

But what Conor really wanted
was to play music
all by himself.

His big sister Laura
could play the piano.
She was very, very good.

She also had an
electronic keyboard.
When she was out,
Conor played on her keyboard.

One day, Mum said:
'That's very good, Conor.
Would you like to
learn piano too, like Laura?'

'I'd love to!' said Conor.
He was so happy!
He was going to learn
to play music, **real** music.

Conor began to go for
piano lessons.
His teacher was Mrs Smart,
a nice, patient woman.

Mrs Smart showed Conor
the notes on the page
and the notes on the piano.

Each key on the piano
matched a note written
on the page.
'Cool!' said Conor.

She showed him
the black notes and
the white notes.

He sounded all the
white ones first.
Then he sounded all the
black ones.
Conor loved the black ones.
They sounded strange.

'You will learn to play
the white ones first,'
said his teacher.

Mrs Smart gave him a red book
with lots of songs in it.
Mrs Smart said:
'These are your **pieces**,
Conor. This is what
you'll learn.'

'You have to practise
your pieces, Conor,'
said Mrs Smart.
'If you want to be good
you need to practise
every day.'

Conor wanted
to be good at the piano,
so he practised every day.

But there was one problem.

The pieces didn't sound
like **real music**.
They were not like
the songs on the radio
or on the CD player.

The pieces were
slow and careful.
The pieces sounded like
little broken bits
of proper music.

**The pieces
were boring**.

And they used only
the **white notes**.

'You'll use the other notes later,'
said Mrs Smart,
'When you can play better.'

Every day, Conor practised
his pieces.
His fingers moved
slowly and carefully.

'That's getting very good,'
said Dad.
'Keep up the good work!'
said Mum.

But, after the pieces,
Conor played
his own music.
He used every note
on the piano.

That is 88 notes!
(Conor counted them.)

Conor played all
the white notes and
all the black notes.

His fingers moved
very, very fast.
They raced up and down
the keyboard like spiders.

Conor was delighted.
Now he was playing
real music.

'That sounds really bad,'
said Laura.

But Conor just smiled and
kept on playing
his own music.

One day, Mrs Smart
made an announcement.
'We are going to have
a concert in the
Town Hall,' she said.
'With a real audience.'

The children were a bit scared.

'I must practise more,'
they all said.

'There will be a prize
for the best performance,'
said Mrs Smart.
'Professor Crotchet
from the College of Music
will be the judge.'

'You will all play
your **best piece**,'
she said.

'I'm going to play
my own music in the concert,'
said Conor. 'Not my **pieces**.'

'You are **not**!' said Laura.
'Mrs Smart said
you have to play a piece
from your book!'

Conor's favourite music was called *Crashing Horses*.
He had made it up himself.

When Conor played
Crashing Horses he thought of
huge white horses
crashing and splashing
in the sea on a stormy day.

'I'm going to play
Crashing Horses at the concert,'
said Conor.

'You should play what
Mrs Smart told you to play,'
said Mum.
'That's right,' agreed Dad.
'Play *Here We Go.*'

Every day, Conor practised
his pieces.
He played *Here We Go*
carefully and slowly.

When he played it,
Conor thought of a
very tired person
climbing up a hill
on a grey winter day.

Then Conor played
Crashing Horses.

When he played that,
Conor thought of
the beautiful horses,
stamping and prancing
in the foamy water
on a bright beach.

'Is that *Crashing Horses*?'
asked Laura.
Conor nodded.

'It sounds like noise,
not music,' said Laura.

The day of the concert
finally came.
Conor put on his special outfit.
Laura smirked.
But Mum and Dad
said nothing.

'Have you got your music,
Laura?' asked Mum.
Laura nodded.
She was playing a piece called
The Fairy Harp.

'What about you, Conor?
Have you got your music book?'
asked Dad. 'The one with
Here We Go in it?'

'Yep,' said Conor.

Mum looked at Dad.
Dad looked at Conor.
They all smiled.

Laura looked out the window.

The Town Hall was
full of people.
Ten minutes before the concert,
everybody sat down.
Mrs Smart's piano students
lined up backstage.

Professor Crotchet sat in the
very middle of the front row.
He was a big round man with
lines on his forehead.

Conor thought the lines
looked like the lines
music is written on.
He thought that the Professor
looked like a **huge note**.

Conor giggled.

'Shhh!' said Laura.

Mrs Smart introduced
each student.

Soon it was Laura's turn.
'Laura is going to play
The Fairy Harp,' said Mrs Smart.

Conor smiled at Laura.

'Good luck, big sis!' he said.

Laura played very well.

It almost sounded like

the music on the radio.

The audience clapped

for a long time when she

had finished.

At last, it was Conor's turn.
'Now, our youngest
student, Conor,
is going to play *Here We Go!*'
said Mrs Smart.

Laura glared at Conor.
'Play the right piece!'
she hissed.

Conor walked on to the stage.

The lights were very bright.

He smiled a big smile.

Then he climbed up
on the piano stool.

'Tonight, I am going to play
my own music!'
said Conor.
'Oh no!' groaned Laura.

Conor closed his piano book
and put it down on the floor.
He took a deep breath
and began to play
Crashing Horses.

His fingers raced up
and down the piano.

The low notes sounded
like hooves
banging against
rocks and stones.

The high notes
sounded like flecks of foam
splashing and bursting
in the sunlight.

Then Conor stretched his legs
down as far as he could.
He held the pedals down
to make the music sound like
waves coming in
and going out.

Then he played the last, quiet
part, where the horses
were tired and walked
slowly home along the sand.

Conor got down off the stool,
picked up his music book,
and walked off the stage.

Nobody clapped.
His footsteps sounded strange
and loud in the quiet hall.

Professor Crotchet walked
on to the stage.
'What an interesting
evening of music
this has been!' he said.

'Now, the prize for the
best performance goes to ...
Laura, for *The Fairy Harp*!'

Everyone clapped and
Laura ran out on the stage
with a very red face.

Professor Crotchet handed her
a silver cup.

'That brings us to
the end of our concert,'
said Mrs Smart.'

'**Wait**!' said the Professor.
'There was a very good
piece of music played here
this evening by Conor.
It reminded me of ... of
galloping horses!'

The audience began
to clap and cheer.
'Well done, Conor,'
said Professor Crotchet.

'Have you a name
for your piece?' he asked.
Conor nodded.

'It's called *Crashing Horses*,'
said Conor.

'**Yaay**!' cheered everyone.

'Hooray for *Crashing Horses*!'

'**Hooray for Conor**!'